The Enchanted forest

Written by John Atkinson
Illustrated by Michael Engel

for AMareta + Mark

Stay happy!

[signature]

NOV. 1999

To Margaret, for showing me the way to the enchanted forest. I met Margaret while travelling for twenty one hours on an old bus across the plains of Argentina. Despite having lost one arm to cancer, and being sixty-eight years old, she had left her family at home in Australia and was back-packing around the world all by herself. When I asked her why she had set out on such an incredible journey, she only smiled and said it was her dream and was something she just had to do.

And to Adriana, for walking with me through the ancient and very inspirational forests in Tierra del Fuego, Patagonia, which is where we were camping when this story came to me.

ISBN: 0-929155-40-8

Published by Windward Books International
CANADA:P.O.Box 2329,Orillia,ON L3V-6V7
USA:P.O.Box 142,Lincoln,MA 01773

Chapter 1

"I think I will go out for a walk," said Tom to his dog named Molly. "Do you want to come with me?"

Molly opened an eye and she looked up at Tom, but she did not move.

"Come on Molly. Let's go."

Molly did not even make an attempt to get up.

"All right then," said Tom. "If I have to, I'll go by myself."

Tom went to the front door and after one last attempt to get Molly to come, he stepped outside and he quietly closed the door. He walked past the neighbor's houses and on down to the local park and he sat under a big tree.

"No one loves me," said Tom to himself.

"I do," said a little voice.

Tom was surprised. He thought he was all alone.

"Who said that?" asked Tom.

"I did," said the little voice.

Tom looked all around, but there was no one there.

"Where are you?" asked Tom.

"I'm right here," said the little voice. "Right here above you."

Tom looked up and there, sitting on a branch of the tree was a little bird. She was mostly grey and she had a beautiful red chest.

"Hello," said the little bird.

"You are talking to me?" asked Tom.

"Yes," said the bird. "My name is Montana."

"My name is Tom."

"Nice to meet you," said Montana.

"I'm going to go for a walk. Do you want to come?"

"Where to?" asked Tom.

"I'm going to the enchanted forest," said Montana.

"I've never heard of that," said Tom.

"I'm not surprised," said Montana. "It's not on any maps."

"Where is this place?" asked Tom.

"It is just beyond the trees at the top of the hill," said Montana.

"Perfect," said Tom. "Let's go!"

3

Chapter 2

Tom was standing with Montana at the edge of a beautiful forest. The trees were as big and tall as any he had ever seen and the leaves were very green. There were some vines hanging down from the branches of the trees and on the ground there were many plants and colorful flowers of all shapes and sizes. Tom admired the beautiful green forest and he watched as a bird flew up from the branch of one of the trees and soared across the sunny blue sky.

"Where are we?" asked Tom.

"We are standing at the edge of the enchanted forest," said Montana.

"I have played here many times but I have never seen anything as green as this before," said Tom.

"Come on," said Montana. "Let's go for a walk!"

And so they entered the forest. As Montana flew down the path, she stopped and she touched every tree she passed and she touched all of the plants and the flowers too. Tom followed behind and he touched some of the trees and after a while he got bored and he did not touch them anymore. Montana flew on and she kept touching everything. Soon Montana stopped and Tom stood beside her.

"Why do you touch all of the trees and the plants?" asked Tom.

"Because I like to touch them," said Montana. "Trees and plants need to be loved too."

"They do?" asked Tom.

"Look around," said Montana. "What is it you see?"

"I see the green of the trees and the vines and the plants and I can see all of the flowers too."

"And when you listen," said Montana, "what is it you hear?"

"I can hear the call of a distant bird," said Tom.

"Listen again," said Montana. "What do you hear?"

Tom stood silently and listened.

"Now," said Tom, "I think I can hear what sounds like a river flowing somewhere up ahead."

"That's good," said Montana. "Now listen again. What do you hear?"

"I can hear what sounds like the wind blowing very gently on the leaves of the trees," said Tom.

"And if you listen one more time," asked Montana.

Tom listened very carefully for a long time.

"The wind almost sounds like voices whispering from somewhere far away," said Tom. "It scares me."

"Don't be afraid," said Montana. "Up ahead there is a clearing. The sun is shining there."

They walked toward the clearing and as they went, Montana touched all of the plants and the flowers and the trees.

6

Chapter 3

"Why is this called the enchanted forest?" asked Tom as they went down the trail.

Montana smiled and said, "Soon you will know."

They walked out from the shade of the trees and into the sunshine. There were some small bushes and on all of the branches there were birds. They were all sitting together and singing their beautiful songs.

"This is called the land of the birds," said Montana.

"I think you will like it here."

"Is this where you live?" asked Tom.

"Yes," said Montana. "This is my home."

As Montana and Tom passed the bushes, the birds sang their happy songs. And then, right in the middle of its song, one of the birds flew up and soared across the blue sky. Soon another and another flew up and soared overhead too. One bird flew over and landed right on Tom's shoulder.

"Hello," said the little bird. "My name is Colorado."

"You can talk too?" asked Tom.

"Of course," said Colorado. "And best of all, I can sing."

Then Colorado sang a beautiful little song just for Tom. The bird sang as loud and as clear as she could and when she finished her song, she smiled. Tom smiled too.

"Thank you," said Tom. "I could listen to you sing all day long."

"You are welcome to stay here for as long as you like," said Colorado. "You can sing along with us."

"I'd like that," said Tom.

"When I'm really happy I like to fly," said the little bird.

"Me too," said Montana.

"Let's go flying," said Colorado.

"Let's go," said Montana.

"Come with us," said Colorado to Tom.

"I can't fly," said Tom.

"You can't fly?" asked Colorado.

"I wish I could," said Tom sadly. "But I'm afraid I can't."

"Have you ever tried?" asked Colorado.

"Many times," said Tom. "There are lots of people who would love to fly, but it is something we just can't do."

"I will stay here with you," said Montana.

"No," said Tom. "You go and have some fun."

"Are you sure?" asked Montana.

"I'm sure," said Tom. "I will watch you fly."

"Okay," said Montana. "I'll be back soon."

"Maybe someday we can sing a song together," said

Tom to Colorado.

"Maybe someday we can fly together," said Colorado.

"I wish," said Tom.

Then Montana and Colorado flew up and soared across the blue sky with all the other birds. They flew up and around and back and forth. They all felt very happy and very free. Tom lay down in the soft grass and he watched the birds fly so high in the sky and as he did, he felt as happy as all the others and he dreamed he was up there flying with his new friends.

Chapter 4

Tom lay in the grass and watched as Montana and all of the birds soared across the blue sky. It looked like such fun and more than anything else in the world, he wished to be up there with his friends.

"I wish I could fly," said Tom to himself.

"You better be careful what you wish for," said a tiny voice. "Your wish just may come true."

"Who said that?" asked Tom.

Tom looked in the bushes and he looked in the grass but there was no one around. How strange? thought Tom to himself. He was sure he had heard someone talk but there was nobody there. He looked back up at his friends flying in the sky and for fun, he made his wish again.

"I wish I could fly," said Tom.

"You better be careful what you wish for," said the little voice once again. "Your wish just may come true."

This time Tom knew he had heard a voice.

"Who said that?" asked Tom. He looked all over the place but there was still no one there.

"Who is talking to me?" asked Tom.

Then he heard a little laugh.

"Who is laughing?" asked Tom. "Where are you?"

"I'm right here," said the tiny voice.

"Right where?" asked Tom.

"Right here," said the tiny voice. "On your shoulder."

Tom looked on both of his shoulders and at first he did not see the lady bug sitting there because she was so small.

"Right where?" asked Tom again.

"Right here silly," said the lady bug.

Tom looked down again and this time he saw the tiny lady bug looking up at him.

"You," asked Tom, "are talking to me?"

"That's right," laughed the lady bug.

Tom looked very carefully at the little bug. Her back

was a bright shade of orange and she had eight black dots on top.

"Your colors are beautiful," said Tom.

"Thank you," said the lady bug. "My name is Lady AnnaLee."

"Lady AnnaLee," said Tom. "What a pretty name."

"Thank you," said the lady bug. "My friends just call me AnnaLee. You can do the same."

"Nice to meet you AnnaLee," said Tom.

"The pleasure is all mine," said the lady bug. "What brings you to the enchanted forest?"

"I have come for a walk with my friend Montana," said Tom.

"I could not help but hear when you wished to fly," said Lady AnnaLee.

"Yes," said Tom. "More than anything else in the world, I wish I could fly."

"Wishes sometimes come true," said the lady bug.

"I know," said Tom, "but it is impossible for me to fly."

"Impossible?" asked the lady bug.

"That's right," said Tom.

"Montana flies quite well, don't you think?" asked Lady AnnaLee.

Tom looked up at Montana soaring in the sky with all

of the other birds.

"Yes she does," said Tom.

"Would you believe me if I told you there once was a day when Montana could not fly," said the lady bug.

"I'd find that hard to believe," said Tom as he looked up at Montana flying so freely across the blue sky.

"And you say you could never fly like her," said Lady AnnaLee.

"I don't have any wings," said Tom.

"Believe what you will," said Lady AnnaLee, "and so shall it be."

When Tom heard these words he looked down from the blue sky and he turned to look at the lady bug sitting on his shoulder. And when he did, he was surprised to see that the lady bug named Lady AnnaLee was gone.

Chapter 5

Montana soon returned and landed near Tom.

"Is everything okay?" asked Montana.

"I can't believe it," said Tom. "I have just been talking with a lady bug."

"Anything is possible," said Montana.

"Anything?" asked Tom.

"That's what I believe," said Montana. "We better get going. I want to try and find the meadow of dreams. I think you will like it there"

"I'm starting to like everything here."

Just as they started to leave, Colorado landed on a nearby branch."

"I hope to see you again sometime," said the little bird.

"I hope so too," said Tom.

"Maybe we can sing a song together," said Colorado.

"I would like that," said Tom.

"I will wait for you," said the little bird.

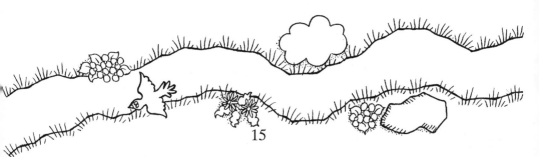

As Montana and Tom moved on, they could hear as Colorado started to sing another of her songs. It was very beautiful and soon all of the other birds landed nearby and sang along with her.

"What a wonderful place," said Tom.

"It is a magical place," said Montana.

At the far end of the clearing they came to a river. It was not a big river but the water was deep and out in the middle there was a small current and the water was flowing softly.

"We must cross this river," said Montana. "Can you swim?"

"I'm a good swimmer," said Tom. "I can swim across this."

"Are you sure?" asked Montana.

"I'm sure," said Tom.

"I'll be nearby," said Montana. "If you need me, just call."

"Okay," said Tom. "Let's go."

Tom walked into the water and soon he was swimming for the other side. At first everything was okay and Tom was having no trouble. But when he got near the middle of the river, he found that the current was stronger than he had first thought.

He tried to swim through the current but he could not. He tried a second time and again he found he just could not make it and after a bit of a struggle, he decided to turn around and go back to where he had come from. Montana flew back with him and soon they were once again standing on the beach by the land of the birds.

"Are you alright?" asked Montana.

"I'm okay," said Tom.

"What happened?" asked Montana.

"I don't know," said Tom. "I should be able to swim across this river but I can't."

Tom stood at the edge of the river and he looked across to the other side and he tried to figure out why he could not get there. But try as he might, he could not think of one good reason why he could not make it across the river.

"What is holding me back?" asked Tom.

Chapter 6

"I should be able to swim across this river," said Tom.

"What is it you are carrying in your knapsack?" asked Montana.

"Just some things," said Tom.

"Maybe you should think about leaving the knapsack here," said Montana.

"I never go anywhere without this stuff," said Tom.

"You might be able to cross over without it," said Montana.

"I just can't leave it behind," said Tom.

"Why not?" asked Montana

"Some of these things are very important to me," said Tom.

"I have an idea," said Montana. "We will leave your bag here by this old oak tree and later we can come back for it."

"Will it be safe here?" asked Tom.

"It's your stuff," said Montana. "No one else wants it."

"If you say so," said Tom.

Tom carefully took the knapsack off his back and he gently put it down by the old oak tree. He placed it in a dry spot where he could easily see it from the other side of the river and after one last look, he turned and he went back to the water's edge.

"Are you ready?" asked Montana.

"I'm a little bit nervous about leaving my bag behind," said Tom. "But I'm ready."

"Are you sure?" asked Montana.

"Yes," said Tom. "To tell you the truth I feel a lot lighter without that weight on my shoulders."

"That's good," said Montana. "Let's go for a swim."

And off they went again. Tom walked into the shallow

water and soon he was swimming and before long he was out in the middle of the river. The current was just as strong as before and this time Tom was ready. He swam as hard and as fast as he could and with no trouble at all he broke through the current and he swam toward the distant shoreline.

Montana flew at his side all the way across the river and soon Tom stood up in the shallow water and he walked toward the shore.

"I made it," said Tom.

"You sure did," said Montana.

"I guess you were right about that knapsack," said Tom.

"If you need it," said Montana, "you know where you left it."

"That's true," said Tom. "But I think I would like to try and get by without it for awhile."

As Tom stood by the river and dried himself in the warm sunshine, he looked back across the river. He could see the old oak tree standing by the water's edge and he could see his knapsack sitting there all safe and sound and after one last look, he turned away and he walked on through the enchanted forest.

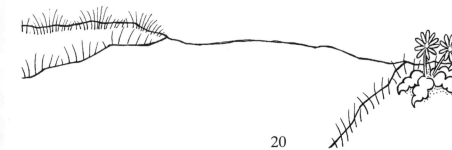

Chapter 7

"How do you feel about leaving your knapsack behind?" asked Montana.

"I thought I would miss it," said Tom, "but the funny thing is that I don't."

Tom looked up and watched as a bird lifted clear of the branches of a tree and winged its way across the afternoon sky.

"Did you always know how to fly?" asked Tom.

"No," said Montana. "I had to learn how to fly."

"Do you think I can learn?" asked Tom.

"It's not up to me," said Montana.

"Who decides?" asked Tom.

"Who do you think decides?" asked Montana.

"I'm not sure," said Tom.

"Soon you will know," said Montana.

They went side by side through the forest. Everything was very green and very beautiful.

"The trees here seem much bigger than the ones we saw before," said Tom.

"They are," said Montana. "These are the oldest and the tallest trees in the forest."

"This seems like a special place," said Tom.

"This is a very special place," said Montana.

"Why is that?" asked Tom.

"This is the home of the ancient ones," said Montana.

"The home of the ancient ones?" asked Tom.

"That's right," said Montana. "These trees have been here for longer than anyone can remember."

Tom looked up at the tops of the trees. They were very tall and their branches reached a long, long way up and to Tom they almost seemed to touch the sky.

"How old are these trees?" asked Tom.

"It's hard to say," said Montana. "I only know they are very old."

"I believe it," said Tom as he looked up at how big and strong these trees seemed to be.

"Let's stop here," said Montana. "Tell me what you hear?"

"I can hear the water flowing at the river," said Tom. "And I can hear the leaves of the trees blowing gently in the wind."

"Listen again," said Montana.

Tom listened again and then, for one brief moment, he heard something very strange.

"I don't believe it," said Tom. "I thought I heard a voice in the wind."

"Listen again," said Montana. "And this time listen with your heart."

Tom listened very carefully and once again he heard the wind blow and in that same moment, he heard a voice whisper a quiet message.

"We are the ancient ones," whispered the gentle voice.

"Someone is talking to us," said Tom.

He listened again and he heard the same thing.

"We are the ancient ones," whispered the voice.

"Is that the wind?" asked Tom.

"It is we who stand beside you now," whispered the same voice. "Do not be afraid."

"It is the voice of the trees," said Montana.

"The trees are talking to us?" asked Tom.

Montana flew up and gently landed on the branch of one of the trees and said, "Yes. You are hearing the voice of the ancient ones. Do you believe what you hear?"

Tom looked up and around at all of the beautiful trees and he suddenly felt very small and he said, "Yes. I believe."

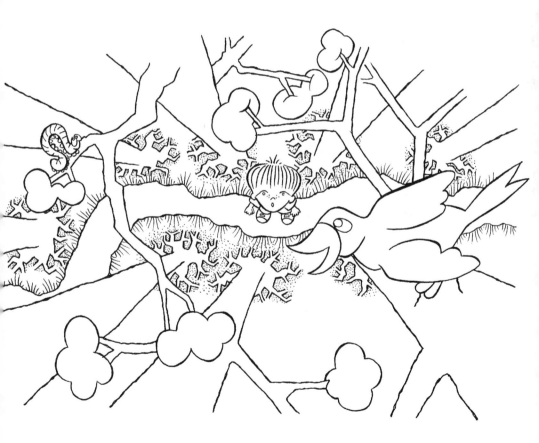

Chapter 8

"You have found your way to the enchanted forest," whispered the voice of the trees.

"Montana brought me here," said Tom.

"We welcome you," whispered the voice.

"We are looking for the meadow of dreams," said Tom. "Do you know where it is?"

"Yes," whispered the voice of the trees. "It is just beyond the valley of darkness."

"The valley of darkness?" asked Tom. "I don't like the sound of that."

"There is nothing to be afraid of," whispered the voice of the trees.

Tom looked up and around at all of the trees and he said, "The trees here are the tallest in the forest."

"There is a reason," whispered the voice.

"There is?" asked Tom.

"Yes," whispered the voice of the trees. "Everything

there is to see, we can see from here."

"What is it you see?" asked Tom.

"Climb up and see for yourself," whispered the voice.

"You don't mind?" asked Tom.

"Of course not," whispered the gentle voice.

"I love to climb trees," said Tom.

The old trees were perfect for climbing. They had many big branches which made it very easy for Tom to quickly climb his way up near the top. Montana flew on ahead and when Tom got as high as he could, he stuck his head out beyond the leaves of the trees and he looked around.

"How's the view?" asked Montana.

"It's beautiful," said Tom.

"What do you see?" asked Montana.

"I can see the blue sky," said Tom.

"That's good," said Montana. "Anything else?"

"The branches are too small and I can't get up high enough to see beyond the other trees."

"We better go down," said Montana. "The branches are very small up here."

Tom was able to go back down the tree just as quickly as he went up and soon he was safely back on the ground.

"What did you see?" whispered the voice of the trees.

"I saw the blue sky," said Tom.

"That is a good start," whispered the voice.

"There is more?" asked Tom.

"Much more," whispered the voice of the trees.

"When do I get to see it?" asked Tom.

"When you are ready," whispered the voice. "You will see everything there is to see."

Chapter 9

Tom and Montana waited for a while but they did not hear any more from the whispering voice of the trees and soon it was time to go.

"We must be on our way," said Montana.

"We have only been in this forest for an hour or so," said Tom, "but it almost feels like home."

"I know," said Montana.

"Do you know how to get to the meadow?" asked Tom.

"Yes I do," said Montana. "But first you must go through the valley of darkness."

"I think you meant to say that first *we* must go through the valley of darkness," said Tom.

"No," said Montana. "First *you* must go through the valley."

"Me?" asked Tom. "Alone?"

"Alone," said Montana.

"And you?" asked Tom.

"I will meet you on the other side," said Montana.

"But I don't want to go through it alone," said Tom. "Why can't we go together."

"It is just not possible," said Montana. "Only one can pass at a time."

"Is there no other way?" asked Tom.

"We can go back the way we came," said Montana.

"I would rather not go back," said Tom.

"We will do what ever you want," said Montana.

"I don't like the sound of this valley," said Tom.

"There is nothing to be afraid of," said Montana. "There is only you, alone with yourself, walking through the valley."

"Have you ever gone through it?" asked Tom.

"Yes I have," said Montana.

Tom thought for a moment and then he said, "Okay. I'll do it."

They stood and they listened to the wind as it ruffled the leaves of the trees and when they continued on their way, the gentle sounds of the wind were all around them.

In a little while the trail turned off to the right and snaked down and under a bent tree.

"The entrance to the valley of darkness is just beyond that bent tree," said Montana.

"I'm ready," said Tom.

"Are you afraid?" asked Montana.

"I am not afraid," said Tom.

"I will be waiting for you on the other side," said Montana.

Tom decided right there and then to be strong. He was not afraid. He would walk through the valley alone. He walked down the trail and he looked back at Montana one last time and then he passed under the bent tree and he entered into the valley of darkness.

"I am not afraid," said Tom to himself.

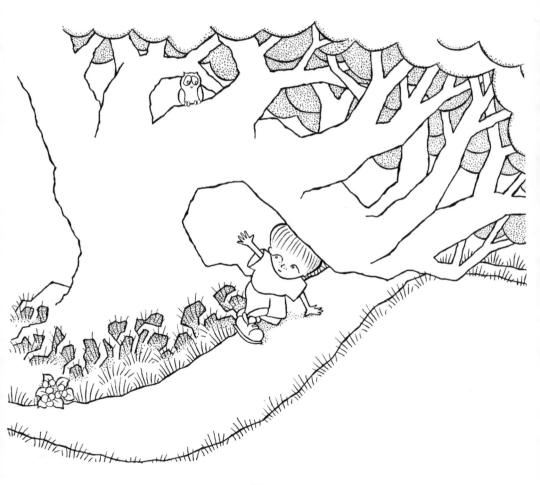

Chapter 10

Tom walked down a hill which led into the valley of darkness. There were many trees along the way and there were lots of plants and flowers too. The sun was high in the sky and there was lots of light and Tom was not afraid.

"I wonder why they call this the valley of darkness," thought Tom to himself.

Just like Montana did before, as Tom walked along the trail he touched and he talked to all of the plants and the flowers and the trees. Whether or not they understood what he was saying was not really important. What mattered was that they made him feel like he was not quite so all alone and he was grateful for that.

He walked along the trail and soon there were more and more trees and because of this, there was less and less sunlight shining down on the trail.

"What lies ahead I do not know," thought Tom to him-

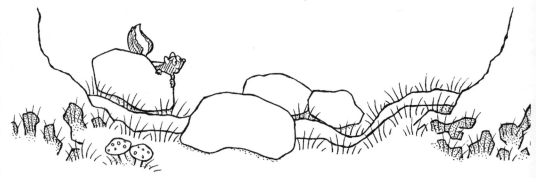

self, "but come what may, I must be strong. If my friend Montana can go down this trail, I can too."

As he walked further and further into the valley, there were more and more trees and soon the trail started to get smaller and smaller. And because there were so many trees, there was not as much light shining down on the trail and soon he could hardly see any of the plants and the flowers along the way. Despite all of this, Tom was determined to carry on.

"I am not afraid," said Tom to himself.

And for awhile he was not afraid. He was very strong.

But soon it got darker and darker in the valley. And then, from off to one side of the trail, Tom heard something move in the bushes and it scared him because he could not see what was there.

"I will not be afraid," said Tom.

He walked on in the fading light and he tried to be strong.

"I am not afraid," said Tom to himself.

Then he heard a wolf howl from somewhere off in the darkness. And he stopped walking. He listened and he heard the wolf howl again. He could not tell from what direction it called and this made him even more scared. No one told me there were going to be wolves, thought Tom to himself. He did not know whether to keep going or to turn around. Were they behind him or ahead of him? Which way should he go?

Suddenly Tom started to think about where he was. He was deep in the valley of darkness. He was all alone. And there were wolves. And it was likely they knew Tom was there. And he didn't know where they were. Then he got really scared. He didn't know what to do. He couldn't move. It seemed like he was frozen in his tracks right there on the trail.

The wolves howled again and to Tom it sounded like they were getting closer and he wanted to run. But he didn't know which way to run. And then he cried out for help. But there was no one there to hear him. There were only the wolves howling. In his whole life he had never been so scared.

"I want to go home," said Tom.

"What is it you are so afraid of?" asked a tiny voice.

Tom spun around on the trail. He thought he was all alone and this unexpected voice spooked him.

"Who said that?" asked Tom.

"It was me," said the tiny voice.

Tom looked all around and much to his surprise, he discovered that he was not alone. Sitting on his shoulder he found his little friend. There he found the lady bug named Lady AnnaLee.

Chapter 11

"Where did you come from?" asked Tom.

"All that matters is that I am here," said the lady bug named Lady AnnaLee.

Tom was standing deep in the valley of darkness. And the wolves were still howling.

"What is it you are afraid of?" asked the lady bug.

"I'm afraid of the wolves," said Tom. "And I guess I'm afraid of being alone too."

"There will be many times in your life when you will feel all alone," said Lady AnnaLee. "In the worst of times you must never lose hope. And

most important of all, you must never stop believing in yourself."

"I tried," said Tom. "But I still got scared."

"Be not afraid," said Lady AnnaLee. "Only believe."

"I'm trying," said Tom.

"Let us go then," said the lady bug. "I will travel with
you for awhile."

And so it was that Tom was able to continue his
journey through the valley of darkness. There was very little
light on the trail and it was hard to see but he kept on
walking. The lady bug named Lady AnnaLee stayed with him.
She stayed right there on his shoulder. And because of her,
Tom felt not quite so all alone. And the wolves did not
howl anymore.

"Can we talk about dreams?" asked Tom.

"I love to dream," said Lady AnnaLee.

"My dream is to fly like
Montana," said Tom.

"That is a good dream,"
said the lady bug.

"When I came to this forest I
was carrying a knapsack filled

with some stuff," said Tom. "And when I took the load off my shoulders, I almost felt like I could fly."

"You probably can," said Lady AnnaLee. "If you try."

"But it is impossible for me to fly," said Tom.

"You are forgetting one very important thing," said the lady bug. "Anything is possible here in the enchanted forest."

"It is?" asked Tom.

"I would never lie to you," said Lady AnnaLee

"Who can teach me how to fly?" asked Tom.

"You mean you don't know?" asked the lady bug.

"Montana said that one day I would know," said Tom.

"And so you shall," said Lady AnnaLee. "The fact is that only you can teach yourself how to fly."

"How can that be?" asked Tom.

"It always comes back to one thing," said Lady AnnaLee. "You must only believe."

"I want to believe," said Tom.

"When you do believe," said Lady AnnaLee, "then you will fly."

"How do I do it?" asked Tom.

"Close your eyes and make a wish," said the lady bug. "And then believe with all of your heart and if it is meant to be, it will be."

Tom closed his eyes and he said, "I believe."

"You must always believe in your dreams," said Lady AnnaLee.

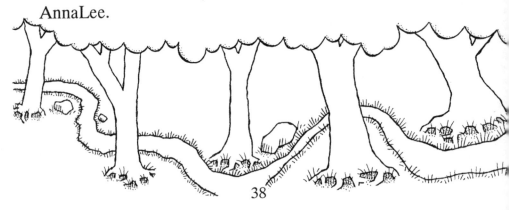

"I believe," said Tom.

"You must always believe that anything is possible, if only you will try," said the lady bug.

"I believe," said Tom.

"Then so be it," said the lady bug named Lady AnnaLee. "You will fly."

Many times late at night, when Tom was sleeping, in his dreams he was able to rise up from his bed and fly over the land and the sea. And now, as he stood in the valley of darkness, Tom wished he could fly just like he did in his dreams. He stood there on the trail and he believed with all of his heart that he could fly. More than anything he had ever believed, there and then Tom believed he could fly in the sky with the birds. He truly believed.

Tom felt a gentle breeze blow through the enchanted forest and in that same moment he felt something strange and wonderful and new come over him and just like in his dreams, he started to feel lighter and lighter and lighter.

The lady bug was herself getting ready to fly and as she spread her little wings, she smiled and she said, "Be not afraid. Only believe."

It was then that Tom felt himself slowly rise up from the ground. He opened his eyes and he saw that he was rising toward the branches of the trees. He was moving up toward the light. Then he passed through the branches and he passed through the leaves of the trees and he moved into the sunshine and he soared like a bird across the clear blue sky.

Chapter 12

Tom was flying! He was soaring up and around and across the sky. Just like Montana, he was flying. He cut through the clouds, he swooped down close to the trees and he flew straight up in the air. He felt wonderful and free and alive. The view from so high in the sky was perfect. He could see the trees and he could see the river and he could see everything which lay beyond the enchanted forest. It all looked very beautiful.

He flew around and around and around. He flew up and down and all around. Soon a bird came along and flew with him and then some others came and joined in the fun and before long a whole flock of birds were swooping and cutting and soaring in the wind with Tom. In his whole life he had never known anything like the sense of freedom he now felt.

Soon Tom knew it was getting late and it was time for him to go and find Montana. After one last flight over the

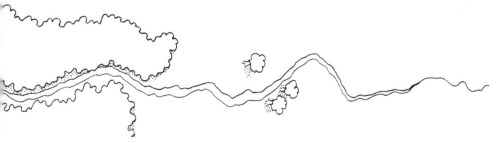

enchanted forest with all of the birds, Tom turned away and flew off to where the valley of darkness ended and he gently landed on the grass by the edge of the trees.

As he stood there on the grass, Tom looked up and he could see the birds still soaring in the wind and he knew now what it was like to fly and a part of him would always be up there flying with the birds.

But there was more. He knew now that it did not matter whether he wanted to build a house or write a book or travel the world or whatever. He could do anything he wanted. All that mattered was that he truly believe.

Then Tom heard the sound of the wind as it blew through the enchanted forest. He listened very carefully as the wind

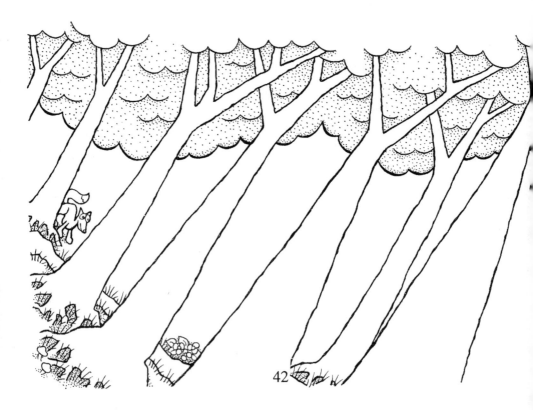

ruffled the leaves of the trees and soon he heard what he was hoping one last time to hear before he had to go.

"We are the ancient ones," whispered the voice of the trees.

"I have learned how to fly," said Tom.

"And what was it you saw when you were up in the air?" whispered the voice of the trees.

"I saw the forest and the river," said Tom. "I saw the birds and the sun and the clouds, and in the distance I saw the ocean and the whales and the dolphins. I saw everything. It almost seemed like I could see forever."

"This is good," whispered the voice.

43

"I felt like I was somehow a part of everything I saw," said Tom.

"You are," whispered the voice of the trees.

"And just like Montana, I wanted to reach out and touch every living thing," said Tom.

"This is very good," whispered the voice of the ancient ones.

"I felt like we were one," said Tom.

"This is the best," whispered the voice. "You have seen the most important thing."

"Yes," said Tom. "Even though I cannot see it with my eyes, I know now that all things are connected."

"This is the one truth," whispered the voice of the ancient ones. "All things are connected."

Then Montana called from the meadow on the other side of the hill and Tom knew that it was time for him to go. That was when the wind blew strong and all of the trees started to sway back and forth. To Tom it looked like the trees were dancing and as he went into the meadow, he danced with the trees as they swayed in the wind.

45

Flying free

From out of the blue
freedom came the other day,
and my ball and my chain
just slipped straight away,
I was standing there thinking
about my worries and woes,
when a little bird came along
and landed right square on my nose.
I didn't flinch, I didn't move
so surprised was I,
when that little bird
looked into my eyes,
I felt that bird
search deep in my soul,
and in that same moment
that bird took control.

She said, "Now is the time
come with me my child,
leave behind all your worries
come with me and fly."
I believed what she said
I believed it was true,
I believed if you try
there's nothing you can't do.
Right then the bird flew off
she soared across the sky,
and when I closed my eyes
I was there by her side,
we cut through the clouds
we soared in the wind,
on that day I felt
like a newborn again.
I was one with the universe
and all things that were,

I connected with the past
the present, the future.
I thank you my friend
for showing me your way,
for teaching me how to live
and be free once again,
in my heart I'm there
right there by your side,
and I'll never forget
how you taught me to fly.

J.C.A.